LOVING ELIZA

Love Detectives

Amy Thompson

About the author

Bestselling author Amy Thompson writes short, exciting, sweet romances. Of course, no romance story is complete without a strong ALPHA MALE who can't live without her and will do anything he can to keep a smile on his queen's face. Sit back, put yourself in a comfortable place, and dive into sweet romantic happily ever after stories.

Be the first to know about new releases, giveaways and other special contents!

Sign up for Amy Thompson's newsletter!

TABLE OF CONTENTS

CHAPTER 1

<u>Eliza</u>

"Eliza, I must commend you for all you've been doing. You've been so good here, and I don't regret employing you at all," Mrs. Smith, the head-teacher, says, stretching her hand out for a handshake.

"Thanks, ma'am," I reply as we shake hands.

She continues, "You have done so well. The students like you, and they won't allow their parents to take them away for any reason. You do know Roselyn is coming back, don't you?"

"Really?" I ask, surprised.

Mrs. Smith nods and smiles. "Yeah, she is coming back. All thanks to you. You know, if it weren't for you, she wouldn't have told her parents to go to California without her. Now her parents have decided that she will stay with her grandmother here in Florida."

"Oh, that's good news. I'm so happy about that, ma'am," I reply, smiling happily. I have been working here as a kindergarten teacher for about six years, and all my students love me.

"With your passion for children and all that concerns them, what do you plan to do? I mean, you don't intend to work here forever, do you?"

I love children, and I would like to own an elementary school of my own. I have been saving up for that, and I know my dream is going to come true someday.

"Well, I would love to own a school too."

"Wow! That's quite interesting, Eliza. You know, when I was about your age, that was my dream too, and I worked so hard to achieve it. Eliza, I love that, and I am so sure you're going to succeed if you focus. Focus is all you need."

"Yes, ma'am," I reply, nodding my head.

Mrs. Smith flashes her teeth at me and reaches for her bag. She brings out an envelope and gives it to me. "Here you go, dear."

I collect the envelope and open it to find a sum of money. I raise my head with a confused look on my face. "I–"

She interrupts, "Don't be scared, dear. I'm not paying you off. That's a sum of $350 from me to you. You've been so good here, and you deserve more."

"Oh, I am so happy. Thank you, ma'am," I say happily.

"It's okay. So, see you tomorrow."

"Yes." I stand up to leave her office. Just when I am about to open the door, she stops me.

"Eliza, focus."

I turn back and smile at her before leaving. It is the end of the day, so I drive straight to the airport to pick my cousin, Jane. The last time I saw Jane was three years ago at my wedding. I will be seeing her today again, and I am so happy about it. She had called last night to tell me that she would be coming to Florida today, and I have to be at the airport to pick her up. Jane is three years younger than I am, but she is a plus-size curvy lady, just like me. We grew up together but had to separate when I came to Florida. As soon as I get to the airport, I rush to the lounge to look for my cousin, Jane.

"Jane, look at you," I say, smiling as soon as I see her waiting patiently in the lounge. We run into each other's arms and hug tightly.

"You've not changed a bit, Eliza. Gosh, you're still hot and gorgeous as ever," Jane says then pulls away from me and holds my hands happily.

"Oh, dear, three good years," I reply, looking at her from head to toe with happiness written all over my face.

"I missed you so much," Jane says and draws me closer for another hug. I help her with her bags, and we go to my car.

"So Eliza, have you found yourself another guy?"

Jane asks while driving to my house. I shake my head then turn to her with a smile on my face.

She continues, "Oh, no. You mean you haven't had another man? You mean you've been all alone for three years?"

I nod. "Huh yeah, I am really in love with my job now and-"

She interrupts, "And you want to get married to your job?"

I nod again, smiling, then turn to look at her. She frowns at me, but I burst into laughter. "So, Jane, tell me about your man. How is he now?"

"Oh, I'm sorry I didn't tell you about it earlier. I broke up with Mark last week, and I had to leave for Florida to get over him. I can no longer deal with seeing him around."

"Oh, I'm so sorry about that, sweetheart. How about your job? I hope this isn't going to affect your job?" I ask worriedly.

"I'm on a month break."

"Okay."

"So you didn't tell me why you guys broke up, I mean you and Lois."

"He was an asshole."

"An asshole?"

"Yeah, he never loved me. We dated for six months before we got married. You know that, right?"

She nods. "Yeah, I do, and you once told me that you were so much in love with him."

"Yeah, I was, but he betrayed me. I never knew during those six months that he was married with kids."

"What!" she exclaims with a big frown on her face.

"Yeah, I found out two weeks after our wedding. He even stole my money."

Jane's face widens with disbelief. "That was so bad. So he only came to steal from you and to betray you?"

I nod. "Yes, dear. Now you know why I am married to my job. I loved him with my whole heart, but he never did."

"Wow! I'm short of words right now," Jane says. "But...but he looked so cool. I never knew he meant danger. You know, when you told me about the divorce, I was so surprised because the marriage didn't even last a month. It only lasted three weeks."

"Yeah, it was only three weeks, and I learned about him in the second week."

"I'm so sorry about that, dear. I thought you broke up because of your job. Everyone knows you love your job so much and will give up everything for it," she says, shaking her head.

"But not as much as I loved Lois back then. I loved him so much, and I was a good wife to him. When I asked him why I deserved such ill-treatment from him, all he said was that he knew I loved him, but he has a family already, and he is never going to give them up for anything."

"Oh, dear. That was so bad. I'm so sorry, sweetheart. I never knew you went through all of that."

"Yeah, and I don't think I want to give any other man a chance-"

Jane interrupts and pats me on the head. "Eliza, you're beautiful. You're hot, and no man is ever going to resist you."

"I know, Jane, but I just want this life that I am living right now. I have no man to worry about and no man to wake up one morning to tell me about his wife and kids somewhere. I feel so secure now, Jane."

Jane nods and takes her hand off my head. "Yeah, I understand, but you have to get one. Alright, I don't want us to talk about your failed marriage anymore. I don't want to keep reminding you of that *asshole*."

She changes the topic to something funny immediately, and we both laugh so hard.

Bryan

It is 7 p. m, and of course, it is the closing hour at work. Today's work was so strenuous, and I am driving straight home now to sleep and prepare for tomorrow. I drive as fast as I can to get to my house. I pull my car to a halt as soon as I get to the car parking lot and step out of the car slowly. As soon as I turn to look towards the door to my house, I see two people sitting comfortably on the doorstep. The last time I had a visitor was only last week, and that was my new house-keeper. *Oh shit!* I turned off the light this morning before leaving, and that is why I can't see them now. I return to my car to bring out my flashlight. I turn it on and point it towards the two figures. I can see a lady and a little girl trying to cover their faces with their hands.

"I'm sorry," I shout and begin to walk towards the door. As I get to the door, my heart skips a beat when I see her. She has on ripped jeans and a small white T-shirt, with her hair dyed red. The first and the only time I saw her was four years ago. I don't even know her name.

"Hi," she greets me with a smile.

"You," I say, still looking at her, surprised.

"Yes. After four years, right?"

I nod my head slowly, not sure if I heard her.

"Be nice to let us into your house."

"Oh, I'm...I'm sorry. Step aside," I say and watch as they both stand up to allow me to open the door. She lights a cigarette and begins to smoke. The little girl next to her starts to cough.

"Shit!" I hear the lady say. She throws the cigarette away while I beckon at them to come inside. Before I offer her a seat, the lady gets comfortable on my couch with a devilish grin on her face.

"So, Bryan," she says. *She still remembers my name.*

"You still know my name?" I ask as I stand with my arms crossed before her.

"Of course, I remember the name of my child's father," she replies. I am so confused right now. I met her four years ago at one of the clubs in Mexico City. I had gone to Mexico to visit my dying mother. I loved my mom so much, but I didn't get to talk to her on her sick-bed. She died right in my presence, and that didn't go so well on me. I mourned for several days before going to a club to have fun and finally get over her death. I drank myself into a stupor that night and spent the night with a call-girl. After having sex, I paid her, and I never saw her again until now.

"I...huh, I don't understand," I say, startled

She stands and wraps her arms around my neck slowly. "I mean, this is your child. What is it that you don't understand?"

"Get off me," I growl and move two steps away from her.

She throws her hands into the air and laughs. "I am so sorry. I didn't mean that."

"It's okay," I reply, looking at her suspiciously. "So, what do you mean by your child's father?"

"Oh. Well, this is your daughter."

"Daughter?"

"Yes, your daughter. I got pregnant that night. Do you remember there was no condom? I found out a month after we met. I tried to get rid of it, but it remained in my womb. I had to wait for nine months to have this child. I had to quit my job for nine full months. Well, I gave her to my grandmother after her birth and continued with my life, but after three and a half years, my grandmother fell sick and could no longer take care of her, so I took her away from my grandmother and allowed her to stay with me for a few months before bringing her to you. I have to get back to work. I am sick and tired of taking care of her."

"You must be crazy. Don't you know what you're talking about?"

"I do know what I am talking about; this little girl here is your child."

I run my fingers through my hair and begin to pace up and down the room with my body boiling with anger. "But you had sex with other men after I left."

"No, I didn't. I swear I-"

"I'm going to ask you one more time. You had sex after that night, didn't you?"

She looks away from me. "Yeah, but that was after a week."

"Yes, exactly what I am talking about here." I stop pacing then turn to look her in the eyes. "You had sex a week after we met. That must be the father."

"No, you're the father."

"I know you're only trying to blackmail me, but please don't try this dirty game with me. I am going to give you whatever you want. Just name it."

She laughs. "I'm going to name it. I want you to take your daughter and allow me to live peacefully."

I turn away from her then turn to look at the innocent little girl sitting quietly on the couch with her eyes fixed on me. "Little girl, your momma here is only joking, and you know what I think? I think you have to return to your father now. It is getting late."

The little girl keeps staring at me without saying a word. I turn to the lady again. "You don't expect me to accept this child without proof, do you?"

She claps and moves closer to me. "She is your daughter. Look at her. She looks so much like you. She has blue eyes just like you."

I shake my head and walk to the door to open it. "I want you out of my house now. It is either I pay you for this bloody blackmail, or you get out of my house and never return."

I watch as she drags the little girl off the couch and begins to walk towards me.

"We will leave, but we will be back soon," she says and walks out of the house with the little girl. *Gosh! Why didn't I use a condom?* I was so drunk that night and didn't use a condom. That child isn't mine, and I am not going to accept whatever she brings just to get money from me. If she wants money, I am going to give it to her willingly, but I am not going to take that child.

CHAPTER 2

<u>Bryan</u>

I get out of bed slowly and go to the bathroom to take a quick shower. I woke up early this morning- about an hour ago. I only slept for about three hours during the night. I stayed awake thinking about the lady that was in my house last night with a little girl, who she had claimed to be mine. I cannot accept the little girl just like that. I don't even know the lady's name. I don't have her phone number or home address. I am sure she is still going to call me for money, and I am ready to give her money, but I am not ready to take that child. *Wait a minute! It's been four years. How did she know I am in Florida? How did she get my home address?* She must be a blackmailer. Drinking isn't my thing. The only time I got drunk was when I had sex with the call-girl, and that was before I started my work here in Florida as a police detective. Now the call-girl has appeared from nowhere after four years to tell me that I am the father of her child. *Impossible! I'm not going to accept that.* Different thoughts ran through my mind all through the night. *What if I am indeed the father of that child? What if the lady decides to go to the Press? The whole world is going to know everything about me.*

After getting dressed, I head outside to my car and drive straight to the station. I am an hour early for work today. I can't wait to see my friends and tell them about what is going on. I am the only one in the office we share now, so I will have to wait till they arrive. I lean comfortably on my seat and begin to close my eyes slowly.

"Hey, buddy," Lucky's voice jolts me awake. I open my eyes wide as soon as I see Rose and Lucky standing before me. I turn to the wall clock and see it is time for work already. I dozed off, and I didn't even know when they entered.

"You didn't sleep last night?" Rose asks, going to her seat.

I scratch my chin and sit upright. "Yes."

"What's the matter?" Lucky asks, still standing before me.

"Guys, I think someone is trying to blackmail me," I reply tiredly.

"Blackmail!" they both exclaim.

"And who could that be?" Rose asks, looking concerned.

"Well, I don't even know her name. Where do I start? Okay. Four years ago, I went to Mexico to visit my dying mom. Unfortunately, we didn't get to talk to each other. She died right in my presence. After her death and everything, I decided to go to one of the clubs there to have fun so I could fully get over my mom's death. I got drunk at the club and had sex with a call-girl. We had sex, and we never saw each other until last night when she showed up at my doorstep with a little girl. She told me that I am the father of the little girl."

"What!" they both exclaim again.

"Yes."

"Didn't you use a condom?" Lucky asks.

I shake my head. "I was so drunk, and I got foolish, and I forgot to use one."

"Jeez," Rose says disappointedly.

"She said she is tired of taking care of the child, so I have to take her while she moves on with her life but-"

Lucky interrupts, "I think that's blackmail, or what do you think, Rose?"

Rose nods. "Yeah, I think so, but at the same time, I think it's not blackmail. What if you turn out to be the father of the child? You had sex without a condom, and this is coming to you like a nightmare now. Did she demand money?"

I shake my head. "No, she said she doesn't want money, but I am sure she is going to come back for money."

"Do you think so?" Lucky asks, looking confused.

I nod and sigh heavily. "Yeah." The room goes silent.

"So can someone tell me about our new officemate?" I say, changing the topic.

"Well, I don't know much about him yet; all I know is that he isn't new in this field. He is from Canada, and he is just like you guys. I mean tall, handsome, macho, and bossy. I got all that information from his picture," Rose says, and we all burst into laughter.

Two hours later, I hear a knock on the door. "Come on in," I say, looking towards the door. A man enters, and I am sure he is the one we've been expecting for weeks- the one who has come to replace Lyon.

"Hi," he greets, flashing his teeth at us.

"Hi, you must be Roy," Rose says eagerly.

The man nods. "Yes, I am."

Rose stretches her hand out for a shake. "You're just exactly what I imagined you to be. I got that from your picture."

"Really?" he asks, laughing in disbelief.

"Our chief has told us everything. He said you'd be here today to take Lyon's place," Bryan says.

"But why do I have to share this office with men? Are there no female detectives?" Rose asks, placing her hands on her hip.

"That's because men are stronger," Roy replies and bursts into laughter. We join him as we watch Rose's angry face.

"Welcome, Roy," I say, smiling at Roy.

"Roy, we are one big family now. I am sure we are going to get along well. To start, we are inviting you over for *Men's Night*. Are you in? Please don't tell me you're married," Lucky says and turns to look at me. I nod and smile at both of them.

"I am not married yet," Roy replies.

"So good to hear," I say happily.

"You've been leaving me out of *Men's Night*. I think I'm going to start *Ladies' Night*, and I'm going to invite Amy and Amber."

We all burst into laughter, but she keeps frowning at us.

Eliza

"Hi, Miss. I am Karen's mother," a woman greets me as soon as I am about to leave the classroom after school.

I stop to look at the tall woman standing before me. "Oh, you're Karen's mother. It is nice to meet you."

"Nice to meet you too, Miss," she says with a smile.

"I'm so happy to meet you. Come on in," I say, and we enter the classroom.

"Yeah, I've been out of town for some time, and I just returned four days ago."

"Okay. So what brings you here? Karen's father has been here to pick her up already."

"Yes, I know. Huh, I just need you to do me a favor."

"A favor?" I ask, confused.

"Yes. Karen's dad and I have been so busy these days, and taking care of Karen with our busy schedule has been so difficult. Huh, so we've decided to bring her grandmother to our house next week to take care of Karen while we are away."

I nod my head. I still don't understand what the favor is.

She continues, "I've met with Mrs. Smith, and she said I should tell you about it."

"Okay, so what is it?"

"Please, I need you to stay four hours after school to take care of Karen. Please, she is all we've got, and she needs proper care. Her dad and I return late every night, and there is nothing we can do to change that."

"Four hours? That's quite a lot."

Mrs. Smith enters and sits next to me.

"The ball is in your court, sweetheart. It is your choice. Remember, this is not the first parent," Mrs. Smith says, looking into my eyes.

Karen's mother isn't the first parent; neither is she the second, third, or fourth. Four other parents have been here to make this same request. Yes, I love kids. I take care of them and teach them, and they like me too, but waiting after school isn't going to work for me.

"It's your choice, Sweetheart," Mrs. Smith repeats.

Karen's mother nods. "I have an idea. How about you take them home, and we come over to pick them up after work?"

"Yeah, I think that's a good idea," Mrs. Smith agrees. "What do you think, Eliza?"

I have no problem bringing the kids to my house, but I have to tell Jane about it first.

"Alright, I'm going to think about it," I reply. Karen's mother smiles at me, and I can see the happiness written all over her face.

Bryan

Tonight's *Men's Night* was awesome with our new friend, Roy, and we all got to know him better and talked about several things. Roy doesn't have a woman yet, and that makes us both on the same page. I am home now after spending about three hours at a bar. I head straight to the kitchen to get myself a cup of water. I hear the doorbell ring just as I am about to take a drink, and my heart skips a beat immediately. I turn to the wall clock- it is 9 p.m. *I hope that isn't the call-girl again.* I walk slowly to the living room to get the door.

"Hi," she says as soon as I open the door.

"You?" I ask, looking at the call-girl and the little girl standing next to her.

"Yes. I told you, didn't I? I said we would be back, didn't I?"

"Why are you here again?" I ask calmly now.

She smiles at me. "Allow us in."

"Not until you tell me why you're here," I reply defiantly.

The little girl sneezes, and I know it must be a result of the cold out here. I step aside and beckon them in. I watch as they walk in slowly and sit comfortably on the couch.

"I'm going to take it easy on you now, Bryan," she starts.

"How?"

"You know, I don't want to force things on you. I understand the fact that you had sex with me, and you never expected me to get pregnant and show up at your doorstep after several years with a little girl that I claim to be yours. Now, I know you don't trust me, but we both have to make this work now for our daughter."

I laugh hysterically and move closer to her. "You mean our daughter or your daughter?"

"Bryan, how about a DNA paternity test?" she asks angrily.

The room is silent now. I am beginning to get scared. I hate the fact that she mentioned *DNA*. I thought she was going to ask for money after proving so stubborn, but now it seems she means business.

I clear my throat and turn to look at the little girl who keeps staring at me. "A DNA paternity test is a good idea, but are you sure you want to do this? I mean, what if I am not her father? You're just going to lose this game."

The corner of her mouth twitches. "You're going to be the loser, Bryan."

"So when do you want us to go to the hospital?" I ask, looking scared now but trying to summon courage.

"Tomorrow morning. I have to return to Mexico as soon as the test result is out."

"Alright, I'll be at FLOD hospital tomorrow morning, waiting."

"Good."

"So, I think we are cool. You may leave now," I say with a fake smile on my face.

The little girl turns to her mother and holds her hand. "Can we spend the night here?"

"No, Dora. We have to return to the hotel now."

The call-girl turns to look at me.

"You can spend the night here if you want, and we are all going to leave for the hospital first thing tomorrow morning," I say, turning to look at the little girl who smiles happily at me.

I have two vacant rooms in my house, so I clean one of them hurriedly and lead them inside before returning to my room.

I can't believe this is happening to me. I hope the DNA paternity test is going to tell me that I am not her father, and it will finally end this shit. If the little girl turns out to be my child, then I am going to be in big trouble. I am not ready to be a dad now; I want a woman first. It sucks to be a dad.

CHAPTER 3

Bryan

Today is another day, and I am so nervous. I slept for only three hours last night, and I am awake now, thinking about what is going to happen today. I get out of bed, leave my room, and walk towards the next room. I knock on the door several times, but there is no answer, so I push the door open, only to find the room empty. I sigh, relieved a bit. *They must have left my house early; the game is over.*

I smile happily and turn to leave the room. As soon as I am out of the room, I see the little girl standing right before me at the door with her hands on her hip.

"Hey, you scared the hell out of me," I say, staring at the little girl.

"Why are you so scared, Bryan? Not even a good morning from you?" she asks with a smile.

I smile back at her and scoff. "Morning, little girl."

She frowns. "I'm no little girl. I am four, and I am a grown-up already."

I burst into laughter. "Who says you're not a little girl?"

"My mom," she replies, folding her little arms across her chest.

"Oh, so I am just going to accept that you're not a little girl. Are we cool now?"

"Yeah," she replies happily.

"So, what's your name?"

"Dora. My name is Dora, but my grandmother calls me Princess."

"Oh, Princess, I think I love that too."

She smiles. "Yeah, but my mom doesn't call me that. I don't like her. She is so mean."

"Oh, no, you don't hate your mom, Princess."

"I don't like her. She is always threatening to throw me into a river if I don't listen to her."

Why on earth would anyone threaten to throw her child into a river? Now, I understand why she said she could not single-handedly raise this child; she is only going to kill her.

"Where is she?"

"She is in the kitchen."

"What? She is in my kitchen?" I rush off to the kitchen to find the call-girl, cooking.

As soon as she sees me, she smiles at me. "Good morning, Bryan. You must be wondering why I'm in your kitchen. Well, I am trying to make Dora breakfast if you don't mind."

I nod my head slowly. "I...Huh, we are running late."

"Yes, I know."

I nod my head again and return to my room to get ready. An hour later, we all leave for the hospital. On getting to the hospital, I walk up to one of the nurses.

"Good morning," the nurse greets, smiling at me. "How may I help you?"

"Huh, I'm Bryan. I need to see Dr. Joe, please."

"Do you have an appointment with him?"

"No, huh, I am here to-"

"Hold on a sec," she cuts me off then puts a call through to Dr. Joe. A few minutes later, the nurse leads the call-girl, Dora, and me to the doctor's office.

"It's good to see you again, Bryan," Dr. Joe starts, smiling at us. "So, what brings you here?"

"I want to know if this little girl here belongs to me," I reply, pointing to Dora.

"So, you're here for a DNA paternity test?" he asks then turns to look at Dora.

"Yes, how much will it cost me?" I reply.

"$200, and if you want the test now, you'll have to follow me to the lab with the little girl."

"Dr. Joe, you don't need to worry about the bill. I'm going to settle that today. The test is much more important to me now," I reply then turn to look at the call-girl sitting next to me.

A few minutes later, Dora and I follow Dr. Joe to the laboratory.

Eliza

"You can bring them in. I love kids and love them around me, Eliza. Having them around is going to be fun," Jane says happily after telling her about my new plan.

"Are you sure you want me to bring them here?" I ask.

"Sure. I am so happy. There are five of them, right?"

"Yeah, just five, but I am sure that number is going to increase later."

"That's great. I'd love to have hundreds of them around here."

"Are you serious? I am going to bring them today. Are you comfortable with them around today, Jane?"

"I am comfortable around them any day and anytime."

I draw closer to her for a hug. "Alright, take good care of yourself."

"I will, dear."

I leave the house for the school happily. On getting to school, I walk down to Mrs. Smith's office to tell her about the good news. She is so happy with my decision.

Bryan

"The result will be out in three days," Dr. Joe says after the test.

"Okay, so we may leave now?" I ask.

"Do you know what I think, Bryan?" he asks, looking at me then turning to look at the little girl. "I think you don't need this test."

"Yeah, I knew right from the start that I don't need this test, and that lady out there is only trying to blackmail me. Dr. Joe, I think we are on the same page now."

Dr. Joe laughs. "No, that's not what I'm trying to say. I mean, she looks so much like you."

My heart skips a beat with fear. "You must be kidding. This isn't my child. I have no child."

"Just take a close look at her eyes; they are just like yours. No doubts."

I glance at the little girl, who bends her head low. "We are all going to wait for the test, doctor. I have to go now."

"Alright, Bryan," Dr. Joe says. Dr. Joe's observation scares me. *Bryan, start preparing for fatherhood.* I leave the lab with Dora walking right behind me. As soon as the call-girl sees us, she comes running towards us.

"Hey, what's up?" she asks.

"Nothing, we are just going to come back for the result. It is going to take three days," I reply. I roll my eyes and shake my head. "I don't even know your name."

"Anita. I am Anita," she replies.

Now I know her name after four years. "Anita, why are you doing this to me?" I ask sadly. I know where all this is going to end, but I don't want to accept it.

"I don't understand, Bryan," she says, looking so confused.

"I mean, why don't we just settle this amicably? Why do we have to come here for a test?"

"Oh, now you know she is your daughter?" she asks, folding her arms across her chest.

"No...yes, I mean, no."

She lowers her voice. "Look, Bryan, I don't wish to force things on you now, but I can't cope anymore. I can't raise this child all alone. I have to return to work."

I sigh heavily. *Who says she is my daughter yet?* The test is not out, so I am not going to accept defeat now. "I have to go now."

"Okay, so we will be back for the result," Anita says then leaves the hospital with Dora. I drive straight to the station and rush down to my office.

"You're late, buddy," Lucky says as soon as I enter.

"Yeah, we had to run the test this morning," I reply, walking towards my table.

"Wow, so soon," Rose says.

I shrug. "Yeah, she wouldn't let me be. She came up with a DNA paternity test."

Roy snorts. "Good thing she came up with that. It is going to clear all doubts."

"Yeah, Roy, you're right. What if our dear friend here turns out to be the father of the child?" Lucky asks then turns to me. I am already preparing to be a dad, but the fact that I am going to be one so soon scares me. I am going to love my kids, but there is this scary part about being a dad.

"I don't want my nightmare to come true. I am not ready to be one now. I swear I am not going to take it easy on her if I find out that I am not the father of that child."

"And it is not going to be easy on you if you find out that you're the father," Rose says, scaring me.

I need someone to pinch me and bring me out of this nightmare- someone to tell me that everything isn't real. I need someone to tell me there is no Dora, nor is there Anita. I don't want this to happen to me now. I don't even know what it takes to be a dad. I don't want to wake up early to get a child ready for school, nor do I want to drive a child to school.

CHAPTER 4

Bryan

The loud buzz from my phone wakes me. I have been sleeping for hours.

"Oh shit!" I murmur and pick up my phone from the little table next to my bed. There is a call from an unknown number. I pick up the call and wait for the caller to start the conversation.

"Hello, Bryan, this is Anita."

"Oh, Anita," I reply slowly. I don't remember exchanging contacts with her the last time I saw her. *How did she get my number?*

"Bryan, I am in the hospital now, and the doctor, I mean your doctor, has refused to show me the test result. What exactly are you hiding from me? Why is your doctor hiding the test result from me?"

"Test result? OMG, it's today. I am so sorry, Anita. I swear I forgot that we are to be at the hospital today for the test result."

"You forgot!"

"Yeah, I am so sorry."

"So, I am the only serious one here, right?"

I jump out of my bed and rush to the bathroom. "I promise I'm going to join you soon."

"I'll be waiting," she says and ends the call while I begin to brush my teeth hurriedly. I am not going to have my bath today, because I don't know what is going to happen if I am late to the hospital. I rush out of the bathroom, get my clothes on as fast as I can, and hurry out of the house.

"Hi," I greet Anita as soon as I see her in the waiting room.

"Hi, can we go to the doctor now?" she asks and starts to walk towards the doctor's office while I walk behind her.

Dr. Joe is about to leave his office.

"Hey, good morning," Dr. Joe greets as soon as he sees us.

"Good morning, doctor," I reply and stretch my hand out for a shake.

"You're so lucky to meet me," he says as we shake hands.

"Yeah, is the test result out?" I ask, smiling at Dr. Joe and waiting for him to tell me that Dora isn't my child.

"Yeah, Bryan, have a seat, please," he says, and we sit before him.

"Where is the little girl?" Dr. Joe asks, looking at Anita.

"She is in the hospital playground," Anita replies.

"She is not ill, is she?" Dr. Joe asks and opens his safe. A few minutes later, he brings out two white envelopes and hands them over to Anita and me. "That's the test result. Bryan, she is your child. You can check the result."

I open the envelope quickly and take a white folded paper out, then turn to look at Dr. Joe with a big frown on my face. "No, I don't believe this."

"Bryan, you have to believe. This hospital is one of the best in town when it comes to a DNA paternity test. Bryan, there is no mix-up. She is your child. You and I have been together for years. You're the only one I know; I don't know this young lady here. If you don't believe this result, then I'll advise you to go to another hospital for the same test just to clear your doubts."

"Bryan, you still don't believe?" Anita asks, turning to look at my sad face.

I remain on the seat, stunned. This is my worst nightmare, and I still need someone to pinch me out of it.

"Doctor, thank you so much for proving me right," Anita says to Dr. Joe.

I stand up slowly and begin to walk out of the office with my head down in disappointment. I walk down to the hospital playground. I see Dora playing and laughing happily with some kids. She seems so comfortable and happy here and doesn't know what I am feeling right now.

I feel a tap on my shoulder then turn around to find Anita standing with her arms folded across her chest.

"What's next?" I ask.

She points to two chairs in the playground, and we go there to sit.

"I am so sorry about everything, Bryan. I didn't mean to bring all of this upon you, but I had no choice," she starts.

"Anita, we can sort this out without affecting either of us," I reply. I just hope she is going to accept this offer and not turn it down. "Anita, I can't do this all alone. I will pay you to take care of this child. I promise I am going to take responsibility, but please don't leave her with me."

Anita shakes her head and clears her throat. "Bryan, don't you get it? I want to return to work. I am a call-girl, and that is how I make my money."

"But I am ready to give you a new life, Anita. Now, this is a better offer for you- I am going to keep your account pumping every month just for you to live well with Dora."

"Being a call-girl is already a part of me, and I don't think I want to give it up for any reason- not even you or Dora. Dora has been hindering me from doing whatever I want, but now that you know she is your daughter, I think I am as free as a bird now."

I sigh heavily then turn to look at the innocent girl playing. "I am giving you a chance to think about it now, Anita. She knows you better than me."

She chuckles. "She doesn't even like me. She doesn't love me, and I regret having her when I wasn't ready to have a child. Dora prefers her grandmother to me, but now her grandmother is ill and can no longer take care of her." She snorts then turns to look at Dora. "I loved her the first day I set my eyes on her, but now I don't like her anymore. I like my job instead."

"But you can't leave me to take responsibility," I say defiantly.

"But you left me for four years to take responsibility, didn't you? How about we go to court to make things right?" she snorts. I remain silent and keep staring at the little girl. The court is only going to make things worse and make the whole world know about me and what I did four years ago. We can settle this amicably without involving the court.

"No, I am not going to accept her just like that. Why not call her and ask her who she wants to go with?" I ask angrily. She looks like she is going to say something but just nods and calls Dora. Dora comes running towards us happily.

"Hello," Dora says, panting.

"Dora, remember I told you that this is your father," Anita starts.

"Yes," Dora replies, nodding her head.

"Now, who would you like to go with? Would you like to return with me to Mexico or remain here with Bryan, your father?"

Dora turns to look at me then turns to look at the kids in the playground.

"I will go with him," Dora finally says, pointing to me. My heart skips a beat.

"Me?" I ask, shocked.

"Yes, she wants to go with you. I think I am free now," Anita says then stands up. "I have to return to Mexico today."

"You're returning to Mexico now? I mean, why are you doing this?" I ask, shocked.

"Why am I doing what? Now we both know that she is your child, and the next step is to accept her. You've got no choice now, Bryan."

I stand up immediately and grab her hand so tight. "Where the hell do you think you're going?"

"Bryan, you're hurting me," she screams, while the kids on the playground focus on us now.

"You're not leaving her with me forever, are you?" I whisper.

"Okay, let me go. I promise I am going to be back soon to check on her." She moves closer to me and whispers into my ear, "You know where to find me if you need me. Mexico."

Hell no! I am never going to have sex with her again; I am never going to get drunk. I watch as she pats Dora on the head and winks at me before leaving the playground. I am dumbfounded, and my feet are too cold to move from the playground. My mind cannot stop spinning with thoughts of being a father without getting ready to be one.

I feel a tap on my hand, and I look down to see the little girl standing next to me.

"Are we leaving here? I want to join them," Dora says, pointing to the kids on the playground.

"You want to join them? No, you can't join them because we are not going to be here forever," I reply with a fake smile on my face.

"No, I want to join them," she squeaks.

"Hey, Princess, don't create a scene here. Alright, I promise to take you out on weekends but not here. I am going to take you to other parks where you are going to find several kids, okay?"

She blinks and nods her head slowly. "Okay."

I smile at her again then stretch out my hand. She stares at my hand for a minute before holding it. We walk out of the playground, then go to the hospital parking lot, and drive straight to my house. I don't know where to start. I can't take her to work, so my house is the best place to take her.

She screams for joy and begins to jump on the couch as we enter the house.

"Careful, Princess, don't get hurt," I warn then begin to search for my phone. Now I remember I left it in the car, so I will have to return to my car to get it. I start to walk towards the door, but stop immediately and turn around. "Princess, I'll be right back. Please don't play rough, please."

"Alright, Dad," she replies then stops jumping. I walk out of the house slowly to get my phone. She just called me *Dad*. It is so crazy, but I love the fact that she called me Dad. I didn't get to see my father; he died the day I was born, so I didn't get a father's love. Now, I have a daughter, and I am beginning to feel proud. *Wait a minute!* I still don't know what it takes to be a dad. I am thirty-four, and I still don't have any woman in my life. The last time I had a woman in my life was three years ago, and I lost her due to my carelessness. I loved Benita so much, but not as much as I loved my job. Benita was ready for marriage, but I wasn't, so she left me. I was so in love with my job then that I gave Benita up for it. Now, I am so full of regret for ever letting her go. I am not craving a woman now because I have a child, but I want to feel what love is. I want to be in love and be loved again after three years, and I am never going to give her up for anything, not even my job. I get into my car and pick up my phone. I dial my new housekeeper's number. It rings several times before she finally picks up.

"Hi, Bryan."

"Hi, Miss Coker, I need your help urgently. I'm sorry this is coming late, but I have no choice now."

"Oh, tell me about it, Bryan."

"We agreed that you're going to start work next week, right?"

"Yes."

"I need you to start today. I'm going to explain everything to you as soon as you arrive. I have a four-year-old girl here, and I can't take care of her alone."

"You never told me you have one."

"Yes, I know. I promise I'm going to tell you about it as soon as you get here."

"I'm so sorry to inform you, Bryan, I won't be able to make it today or tomorrow. You know we agreed to meet next week, so I got another job for this week."

I sigh, disappointed. Miss Coker is the only option I've got right now. I don't have a family member here in Florida; they are all in Mexico, and they are all busy with their work and families.

"Bryan, are you there?" Miss Coker's question brings me out of my thoughts.

"Oh, I'm sorry, yeah."

"I said you should enroll her in school."

"Yeah, I think that's a good idea."

"I have to go now, Bryan. I'm going to call you later. I have to attend to something immediately."

"Alright, thank you."

Miss Coker disconnects the call. Oh, *I'm running late for work already*. My phone starts to vibrate- there is a call from Lucky. I pick up immediately.

"Morning, Lucky," I greet.

"Morning, buddy, why aren't you at work yet? Are you still in bed?"

"No, Lucky, huh, I'll be coming late to work today. The test result is out."

"What!" he exclaims over the phone. "So, who is the father?"

I sigh then sit back on the car seat with my eyes closed. "I am."

"OMG! What do you plan to do now? I mean, this is crazy, man. Tell me the child isn't with you now."

"She is in the house with me. We just got back from the hospital. Her mother left."

"What!" he exclaims again. "Shit! You shouldn't have allowed her to leave without the child."

"There was nothing I could do at that moment. I was so shocked when I heard that she is my daughter."

"Oh, God, this isn't happening."

"It is, Lucky. What do I do now? The little girl is in my house right now, and I can't go to work with her. I can't leave her here."

"Hold on, Bryan. I want to hand the phone over to Rose. She has something to say."

I wait till Lucky hands the phone to Rose.

"Bryan, are you okay?" Rose asks, clearing her throat.

"I'm trying to be."

"Good. Now, you have to enroll her in school immediately. You can't keep her in your house all day, nor can you bring her here. You have to get her enrolled in school immediately, Bryan."

"I don't have any. I mean, I don't know any school."

Rose snorts. "Wake up, Bryan. There are several schools around you. All you need to do is find one and get her enrolled."

"Alright, Rose, I will," I reply, sadly.

"Good, Bryan. So, do that now and be here soon, okay?"

"Okay," I reply then disconnect the call. I hop out of my car and rush into the house to find Dora fast asleep on the couch. I move closer to her and sit next to her. She is so beautiful and innocent. Indeed, I am not ready for fatherhood, but I am ready to give this little child a good life- a life that she deserves. I have to accept her fully now as a part of my life. She sneezes and opens her eyes slowly.

"You're awake, Princess."

She scratches her eye with her little finger and yawns. "Yes."

"Get up. We have to get you in school now."

She nods her head happily. "I'd love to go to school."

"Yes, Princess, we have to move now."

She hugs me happily while I pat her on the back slowly. A few minutes later, we leave the house and drive to Avacado, a street about twenty minutes from my house. I begin to look from left to right for a beautiful elementary school. I finally see one after searching for about ten minutes. We hop out of the car and walk into KB Elementary school. There are kids about Dora's age in the school playground, and I know by her smile that she is going to like this place.

"Hey, how may I help you?" I hear a man ask. He is in uniform, and there is no doubt that he is the security-man here.

"Hi, my little Princess is new here, and she likes this school. I want her enrolled," I reply, looking around the beautiful environment.

"Oh, follow me," the man says with a smile and leads us to a small building next to the playground. Soon, we enter an office and find a middle-aged woman.

"Ma'am, they are here to see you," the man informs the woman.

"Oh, you're welcome. Please sit," she says and stretches her hand to the chairs before her while we take our seats.

"Thanks," I say.

"How are you, cutie?" she asks Dora with a smile on her face.

"I'm good," Dora replies sharply.

"Huh, my name is Bryan Sandwich, and this is my daughter. I like this school, and I'd love to get her enrolled here."

"Oh, that's good to hear. I'm Mrs. Smith," she says and stretches her hand to me for a handshake.

"Nice to meet you," I say, smiling as we shake hands.

She continues. "You want her to join today?"

I nod my head. "Yeah, I have to get to work as soon as I can and come back for her later."

"What do you do for a living, Mr. Sandwich?"

"I'm a police detective," I reply and bring out my ID card for her to see. She nods her head as soon as she sees the card.

"Okay. There are some steps you will have to take to get her enrolled. First, we need her medical fitness certificate and the fees. I'm also going to give you a list of all she is going to need here as a student. You need to see her class-teacher and-"

I interrupt, "Yes, ma'am, I know all of that, and I promise I am going to do all of that before the end of this week."

"Alright, don't bother about the medical fitness certificate. We are going to take her to the school's hospital for that," she says.

"Yeah, that's better," I reply, relieved.

"But you have to see her teacher. You have to know more about all you need to do. You have to explain the nature of your job to her and give her a specific hour you're going to come to pick her up every day."

"Yeah, I'm going to do that, but not today. I am late for work now. Can I have the school's account details, so I can make payments?"

"Huh, I'm going to give you the account details but do not send money to it until her medical fitness certificate is out."

"Alright, thank you. I have to leave now. I'll be back by 5 pm."

"School closes at 3 pm today."

"Okay, I promise, I am going to be here at 3 pm," I say and stand to leave, but she stops me.

"Can I have your phone number, your home address, and work address?"

I give her my number, my home address, and my office address. With the office address I provided her, she calls one of the detectives at work to confirm that I work there. We shake hands when she finally finds out that I am real and the information I've provided is genuine. I leave school for work.

Eliza

"Good boy," I commend little Tom as he places some books into his bags neatly.

"Tom has shown you how to arrange your books into your bags neatly. Can you all do that too?" I ask the kids in my class as they watch Tom arrange some books into another bag.

"Yes, Miss Hally," they all reply at once. A few minutes later, Mrs. Smith enters with a cute little girl. They both walk towards me.

"Eliza, this is Dora, and she is new here. She is going to be one of your students."

"Wow!" I bend to look into the little girl's eyes. "Hello, little princess, how are you?"

"I'm good," she replies shyly.

I stand up then turn to Mrs. Smith. "Where are her parents?"

"Her dad was here a few minutes ago, and he will be here to pick her after school."

"I'd like to meet her parents, but I'm not sure I'll be able to meet with them today."

"Why?"

"I'll be leaving at 2:45 pm today to get the kids to my house."

"Oh, yeah, I'm so sorry. I forgot you'll be starting your second job today. You'll be going home with five kids, right?"

"Yes."

"Good. Huh, hopefully, you're going to meet her dad tomorrow morning or next. She is just going to remain in my office after school and wait till her father returns."

"Okay, that'll be great," I reply happily and turn to Dora again. "Welcome to school, sweetheart."

She blushes and begins to look at the other kids in the classroom. Mrs. Smith leaves the class while I lead Dora to join the other kids at their table. I am so happy about this newcomer, and it makes me love my job the more; having more kids around has always been my dream and joy. I'd love to have kids of my own but not with the wrong man.

CHAPTER 5

Bryan

"Hurry, Princess, you're running late for school, and I am running late for work," I shout then peep through the keyhole on the door to Dora's room.

"Give me just a few minutes, and I'll join you," she replies, getting her dress on. She still doesn't have a school uniform. Mrs. Smith, the headteacher, has promised to get her one after I have done everything required of me to get her enrolled in the school. I leave the door then head straight to the kitchen to make breakfast. A few minutes later, Dora joins me.

"How do I look, Dad?" she asks, raising her hands for me to see her dress.

"You look beautiful as ever, my Princess. You're the most beautiful girl in Florida," I reply then move closer to her to buckle the little belt around her waist properly.

She blushes. "Dad, someone else at school calls me Princess."

I chuckle. "And who is that? I am so jealous. Who else calls you Princess here in Florida?"

"My teacher calls me Princess. I like her so much. She is Miss Hally."

"Wow! That's so good to hear. I'm happy you're getting along at school."

"Yeah, and I like the kids in my class too, but they don't call me Princess. They all call me Dora," she says with a frown on her face then smiles again. "Miss Hally taught us how to arrange our books into our bags without anyone's help."

"Wow! I love that, and I am sure you're going to learn more."

"Yeah, so Dad, when are you coming to see Miss Hally? You have to meet her," she says sadly.

"Yeah, I have to. I'm going to see her today. Are you happy now?"

She jumps for joy and pulls me closer for a hug. "Yes, Dad, I am super happy."

A few minutes later, I serve us breakfast, and we both eat hurriedly before leaving the house.

I pull my car to a halt in the school's parking lot, and we hop down and head straight to Mrs. Smith's office.

"Good morning, it's good to see you again," Mrs. Smith greets as soon as we enter her office.

"Good morning, ma'am, how are you today?" I ask, smiling.

"Oh, I'm fine. Thank you. I'm sure you're here to see her teacher, right?"

I nod my head. "Yeah, I am. I couldn't make it yesterday, and I'm so sorry about that. I wanted to see her, but unfortunately, she already left."

"Yeah, school closes at 3 pm, but she closes early with some kids. She takes some kids to her house to take care of them until their parents return in the evening."

"Wow! That's good. I should see her and tell her about the nature of my job too. I would like her to help me with Dora also because I work late as well."

"Well, you should meet with her first and tell her about it. I'm not in the right place to tell you if she is going to accept or not."

"Oh, I'll meet with her," I reply.

Mrs. Smith turns to Dora. "Dora, aren't you supposed to be in class now?"

"No, I want my dad to come along with me. He is going to leave without seeing Miss Hally. I am not going to class without him," Dora replies defiantly.

Mrs. Smith burst into laughter. "She doesn't trust you, Mr. Sandwich."

I turn to Dora, who folds her arms across her chest. "I'll go with you, princess."

A few minutes later, Dora leads me out, and we head to her class.

Eliza

"Good morning, class," I greet my students and start to count them. Someone is missing and that someone is the new student. A few seconds after counting, I hear a knock on the door.

"Come in, please," I say. The door opens, and Dora enters with a tall, macho, handsome man. A spicy woody fragrance that spells seduction fills the air as he enters. He looks so familiar. It is apparent that he is taller than me, and he is my type of man. I am beginning to picture the broad chest hiding under the red shirt.

"Hi, it's you," the man says and stretches out his hand for a shake with a big smile on his face.

"Yes, have we met before?" I ask and keep staring at him with a confused look on my face.

"Yes, we have. We've met twice. We met at Lucky's wedding and-"

I cut in, "And Amy's wedding." I take his hand for a shake.

He nods his head happily. "You're correct."

"Wait a minute! Are you Dora's dad?" I ask and turn to look at Dora, who nods her head happily.

"Yes, I am," he replies.

"Oh, this is so wonderful. I mean, she looks so much like you. So, you're-"

He cuts in, "Bryan. I am Bryan, and you are?"

"Eliza."

"Yeah, now I remember. It is so good to see you again."

"It's so good to see you too, Bryan."

"Hold on," I say to Bryan then take Dora to her seat before returning to Bryan. "I am so happy to meet you again, Bryan. I mean, I never knew you're her dad."

"Yes, I am the lucky dad," he says and laughs.

"That's so great. Now, I'm going to give you a list of what she will need here and the time you have to pick her up every day."

"Okay."

"I'm so sorry. Please take a seat," I say and point to a chair. He goes to sit, and I join him. "So, Mrs. Smith has told me about the nature of your job."

"Yes, Eliza. It's so good to know that you're her teacher. It is going to make things so easy for me."

I smile again and begin to wonder why he said seeing me is going to make things easy for him. *Please don't tell me you want me to take her to my house after school.* I keep staring at the handsome man before me. He has beautiful eyes, and his smile is so heavenly, and no woman is ever going to resist him. He is so charming.

"Mrs. Smith told me about your second job. She said you take some of your students home and-"

I cut in, "Yes, and you want me to do that for you too?"

I hear him sigh heavily. "Yes, I...it's not easy for me to pick her up every day at three because I work late."

"Well, that's not a problem, but you have to give me a specific time that you're going to pick her up, and you must keep to that time."

"Yes, I promise I am going to stick to the time. I am going to pick her up every day at six."

"Good. So when do you want me to start?"

"Today," he replies eagerly with happiness written all over his face. I am not planning to turn my house into a school, but I don't want to turn him down. It is so odd to hear, but I want to keep seeing him every day.

"Alright, I'm going to give you another list for that."

"Eliza, money isn't going to be a problem. I am so happy to know that you're finally taking the burden off me, and you're making things easy for me. Thank you so much, Eliza," he replies happily.

"It's okay, Bryan. What about her mother?"

"Her mother," he pauses for a moment then continues, "we are not together. Her mom is in Mexico."

"Oh, I see, so you're the only one left to take care of her now."

"Yes, I am."

"Wow! I know how stressful that can be."

I give him a list of what he has to get for Dora. A few minutes later, we exchange numbers, and he leaves the class.

Bryan

I leave the classroom and head to the school's parking lot, get in my car, and start to drive to work. As I get to work, I hop out of my car and head to the office. The lady I saw a few minutes ago is gorgeous. I want to see her again. I think I am beginning to enjoy Dora's stay in Florida, because, without Dora, I wouldn't have had the opportunity to see her sexy teacher. Eliza is just like Amy and Amber; she is a plus-size, curvy lady. Her eyes are chocolate brown, and she looks too perfect to be behind the four walls of a classroom. I did see her at my friends' wedding, but I didn't notice her as I did back in her class. When I saw her during the wedding, I never thought I'd set eyes on her again. *I guess fate is about to change things now.* I think I am beginning to fall in love again; love at first sight. No, we aren't seeing each other for the first time, so I'd rather call it love at third sight.

"Bryan, what's up? You look so excited this morning," I hear Roy say as I enter the office.

"Yes, he looks so happy this morning," Lucky adds.

"Wait a minute! Has the call-girl come to pick up her child?" Rose asks, concerned.

I shake my head and smile at them. They all wear curious looks on their faces, and I can't wait to spill it out now. "Do you guys know Eliza, Amber's friend?"

Rose and Lucky nod their head while Roy has a confused look on his face.

I continue, "Roy, you're new, and you've not seen Eliza. Eliza is Amber's friend."

"Oh, okay, so tell us about her," Roy says curiously.

"Well, Eliza is Dora's teacher," I finally spill it.

Rose folds her arms across her chest, and with the look on her face, it is apparent that she wants to know more.

"That's great, but what has that got to do with Dora?" Lucky asks.

I chuckle. "That's great news. I mean, having your friend as your child's teacher is so great."

Rose rolls her eyes and shakes her head. "Bryan, you're so funny, but I still find it hard to laugh at you. Why do you think she is your friend? I mean, you guys didn't know each other before the wedding or after the wedding until now, and that's because your daughter is in her school. This is only a coincidence, and she isn't your friend yet."

"Rose, I think this isn't a coincidence," Lucky says then turns to me. "Come to think of it, these days, everything has been happening in a twinkle of an eye. First, a call-girl appeared at your door-step with a little girl she had claimed to be yours, and now you're happy because you saw Eliza. I mean, there is something special about this happiness of yours."

I chuckle again. "Lucky, I know what you're driving at, but trust me, no strings attached. Eliza is just my daughter's teacher and nothing more."

"Are you sure you're not beginning to fall in love with her?" Roy asks and winks at me.

"Huh, I," I pause. I don't want to decide now. I like Dora's teacher, but I want to be sure of my feelings first. "I don't know."

"Hey, buddy, I know that feeling," Roy says then moves towards me. He puts his hands on the table before me and looks into my eyes. "Bryan, think about it. I believe in love at first sight, but I want you to think about it. You should know what you want, and you should go get it as soon as you can."

I nod my head slowly. Roy is right- I have to find out what I want, and I have to pursue it. *Am I falling in love again? - I'm going to find out.*

After work, I hurry straight to Eliza's house, which is close to the school. I knock on the door several times, but there is no answer. I look down at my watch; I am an hour late. I didn't keep my promise, and I feel so bad about that now. I knock on the door again, but there is no answer. *Or am I at the wrong house?* I move four steps backward to take a look at the number on the house again. I am at the right house, and there is no mix-up. Just when I am about to dial Eliza's number, I see a car park right behind my car. A few seconds later, the door opens, and Dora comes running towards me.

"Daddy," she shouts.

"Oh, Princess," I reply happily then bend forward with my arms open wide. She runs into my arms, giggling. I look up to see Eliza and another beautiful lady walking towards me.

"Hi," Eliza greets with a smile on her face. "You're an hour late, Bryan."

"I'm so sorry, Eliza. I tried to keep to time, but I couldn't make it," I reply.

"She's the only one left. The others left about two hours ago," Eliza says then turns to Dora.

"It's not going to happen next time, I promise," I assure her.

"Alright, Bryan, meet my cousin, Jane. Jane, meet Bryan, Dora's dad," Eliza introduces while I shake hands with Jane.

"It's nice to meet you, Bryan," Jane says, smiling at me. "And you've got a smart daughter. I like her."

I blush then look at Dora, who keeps smiling at me. "Thanks, Jane. It's nice to meet you too."

"Do you mind coming in?" Eliza asks, pointing to the door.

I shake my head. "No, we will just leave, and we will see you tomorrow."

"Alright," she replies. We say goodbye to each other, and I begin to walk towards my car with Dora next to me. I open the door for Dora to enter. As I am about to enter the car, I feel Eliza is still standing at her door, staring at me. I turn around immediately, and I find her standing and staring at me with her hands on her broad hips. She waves her hand quickly with a big smile on her face before finally walking into the house. I enter my car and drive back to my house, feeling elated.

CHAPTER 6

<u>Eliza</u>

It's been three weeks, and I've not missed seeing Bryan because he is at the school every morning to drop off Dora. No day goes by without setting my eyes on Bryan. I am beginning to fall in love with him, but I still find it hard to believe that I am falling in love again after promising myself it would never happen again. There are a lot of things I don't know about Bryan yet, but I will be happy to know everything about him. Ever since I got divorced, I have not felt this way with a man, and I have never fallen in love with any man. I have always been serious about my job. I turned every man that came my way down because I thought they were all assholes like my ex-husband. Bryan had come to my house yesterday to pick his daughter, and with the way he looked at me, I can tell he feels the same thing I am feeling right now. Nowadays, I find it hard to look straight into his eyes because it keeps the fire of love burning in me ceaselessly. Right now, I remember Bryan, and the thought of him is making me smile. After his first day at the school, I've loved looking at him. Bryan is just too handsome to resist. I want to keep seeing him every day; I want to feel loved by him. I try to get this romantic fantasy out of my head, but I find it difficult to. *Could this be love? What if it turns out to be that Bryan only admires me with no strings attached?*

"Why are you smiling? Is it something I need to know?" I hear Jane ask, and I lift my chin in her direction to find her standing with her hands on her hips and a little frown on her face.

I blush then shake my head. "Nothing, it's nothing."

"What do you mean, Eliza?" she asks, moving towards me. "I know what it means for a lady to wake up one morning with a smile on her face like she has just seen Prince Charming." I move away from her and start to pace back and forth in the room.

Jane continues with a smile on her face, "Eliza, I know what's going on. I know you like Bryan, and he likes you too. I noticed that yesterday when he came to pick Dora."

"You're right, Jane, but I am so scared. I don't even know what I feel right now. What if Bryan doesn't like me in return?" I finally spill it.

"He likes you. I saw it," Jane replies with widened eyes. I hear the doorbell ring. Today is Saturday, and I am not expecting any parents here until Monday. The last time I saw my students was yesterday, and the next time I will be seeing them is next Monday.

"Are you expecting someone?" Jane asks.

"No," I reply then walk towards the door. As I open the door, I see Bryan standing with a paper bag in his hand.

"Morning," he greets, smiling at me.

"Morning," I reply, surprised. I beckon at him to come in, but he shakes his head and keeps smiling at me.

"No, I'll be leaving soon. I'm just here to drop this off," he says then hands the paper bag over to me. "Dora said I should get her teacher something, and here it is."

I smile then open the paper bag to find a small box in it. *What could be inside the box?*

I close the paper bag then raise my head to look at Bryan. "Thank you so much. You know you shouldn't have done this but-"

He cuts in, "Dora's wish."

I smile again. "Tell Dora that I love her so much. Will you do that for me?"

Bryan nods his head then chuckles. "Yes, I will. I have to go now."

"Alright, Bryan," I reply happily. He waves his hand then turns to leave. He takes five steps away but stops immediately and turns around like he forgot something.

"I forgot to tell you, Eliza, you look beautiful," he says with a smile on his face before returning to his car. With blush on my cheeks, I watch him drive off. I continue to smile with my legs still in the same spot. I know that I am beautiful, but hearing it from Bryan makes me feel so happy. I feel a tap on my shoulder. I turn around to see Jane standing with a curious look on her face.

"Prince Charming has just left. I saw everything through the window," Jane says and winks at me. I roll my eyes and shake my head. She holds my hand, and we both return inside.

"He got me a gift," I say, opening the paper bag and taking out the little box. Jane moves closer to me then collects the box from me.

Jane continues, "What is in this magic box? Let's check it out." Jane unties the bow on the box and opens it to reveal a bottle of perfume.

"OMG!" I exclaim as I see the name written on the bottle of perfume- HER. "How did he know that I've been craving this?"

Jane raises her head to look at me with a frown on her face. "You've been craving this?"

I nod my head quickly and collect the bottle from her. "Yes...yes, I've been craving this. How did Bryan know that I have always wanted this?"

"I don't understand what is going on. Your love story is beginning to drive me crazy. First, Bryan shows up with a box of perfume, then it turns out to be that you have always craved this perfume," Jane says, shaking her head.

"You don't get it, Jane. I can afford HER, but I've always wanted it as a gift, and no one has ever given it to me- not even my ex-husband."

Jane widens her eyes. "Wow, that's so sweet. You know, if I knew you loved HER, I would have given it to you before anyone else. I am so jealous, but how did he find out?"

"Yeah, that's the point. How did Bryan find out that I've always wanted this? My ex-husband didn't even get me this. He never knew that I've always wanted to have this."

My phone beeps, and I unlock it to find a message on it; it is from Bryan.

Hi, beautiful, I hope you like the little present. How about we go out on a date tonight at KB Restaurant? Please don't say no. One more thing- please send me a message as soon as you get this.

Bryan

"He wants me to go out on a date with him tonight," I say excitedly.

"Wow! Sweetheart, I am super-happy for you," Jane says happily.

"I am happy as well, Jane."

"I knew something like this was going to come up. I knew this is all going to end well."

I've always wanted this moment with Bryan- the moment when Bryan would ask me to go out with him. I tell Bryan that I will be going on a date with him tonight, and a few minutes later, I receive a message from him telling me the time for tonight's date.

Bryan

I am in KB restaurant, looking at my watch several times and looking at the doorway. *Has she changed her mind?* It is 8:15 pm, and she promised to be here at 8 pm, but now she is nowhere to be found. I have ordered dinner, and one of the waitresses told me a few minutes ago that dinner is ready. I look down at my watch again. Just as I raise my chin to look at the doorway again, I see her- she is in a beautiful purple dress that reveals her curves and her cleavage. Her blonde hair is brushed and pulled into a ponytail, and the smile on her face brightens the whole room. *She looks perfect.* I stand with a smile on my face as she walks towards me. "You're beautiful as always, Eliza," I say then beckon at her to have a seat. She keeps smiling as we both sit. I can't keep my eyes off her beautiful eyes.

"I like this place, Bryan," she starts, taking her eyes off me to look around the room. "This is my first time here."

"Wow! I'm glad you like it."

She nods her head then turns to me again, still maintaining her smile. The waitress comes to our table with our food and wine, and we begin to eat. There is a thick silence between us, and I hear the soft music from the dance-floor.

I try not to stare at her cleavage because staring at it gets my cock hardening in my pants, so I turn my gaze to the food before me. I clear my throat to break the silence between us. "You must be wondering how I learned your love language."

She stops eating then turns to me with a confused look on her face. "Have you been stalking me?"

I continue, "I checked your FB profile, and I got all of that from it. You like HER, and you've always wanted it as a gift. When Dora came up with the idea of getting you something, I decided to get something so special, something you've always wanted."

"That was so sweet of you. Thank you."

"Don't mention it- anything for an angel like you."

She chuckles. "So Bryan, tell me something I need to know about you and Dora's mother."

I sigh heavily then look straight into her eyes. Her eyes keep me wondering if I have ever seen such a beautiful lady. "Well, I am not married. I had Dora out of wedlock, but now I like the fact that she is already a part of me. I hate telling this story, but I've got no choice now."

"Oh, Bryan, it's fine if it is something you don't want to tell me. You don't have to tell me if it is personal to you."

I shake my head then smile at her. "It's okay, Eliza, I'm going to tell you everything." I can tell she's nervous, so I continue, "Dora's mom is a call-girl I met four years ago; I got drunk, and I had sex with her and never saw her again until a few weeks ago when she showed up at my doorstep with Dora. The DNA Paternity test proves her right- Dora is my child."

Eliza opens her mouth, agape with a sad look on her face. "I'm so sorry about that."

"It's nothing. As I said, I like the fact that Dora is in my life now. If it weren't for Dora, I wouldn't have met you again."

She blushes then looks down at the table shyly. After eating, she talks about herself and her failed marriage.

Who would cheat on such a beautiful lady like her? Her ex-husband was an asshole!

We talk about several things that got us both laughing, and I am so happy she is here with me and keeping a smile on her face. I want to see her again. I feel like placing my lip on hers and feeling the bliss of her lips. I want to feel every part of her body. I don't think I can do without seeing her again.

We leave the restaurant, and I lead her to her car.

"Thank you so much, Bryan. I had a nice time with you," she says then opens the door of her car. She is about to enter her car, but I grab her hand.

"Thanks for coming, Eliza. There's one more thing I have to tell you; you're not coming with your car next time. I'm going to pick you up myself," I say before letting go of her hand. She nods her head. She doesn't move- we are both standing before each other now and staring at each other's eyes in silence. Different things are running through my mind; I want to set my lips on hers, but I'm not going to do that now. I want to take it easy on her. I am not even sure if she likes me or not, so I'm not going to screw things up now. She clears her throat to break the awkward silence between us then enters her car. I wave at her and watch her drive off. I return to my car slowly then drive straight to my house. It is late, but I've got no worries; Miss Coker, my new housekeeper, has decided to take care of Dora whenever I am away.

CHAPTER 7

Eliza

My date with Bryan is one I will always remember. Yes, I am beginning to fall in love with him, and I am ready to give him a chance if he asks me out. That night, I wanted to pull him closer for a kiss, but I couldn't because I felt it was going to be odd, especially if he doesn't have feelings for me, and if he does- good for me. Today is Monday, and I am at school waiting for Bryan to come with Dora. A few minutes later, Dora enters with a woman. I haven't seen this woman before. Bryan had told me that he has a housekeeper who has offered to take care of Dora while he is away, but this woman I see now doesn't look like one. I have always imagined his housekeeper to be an older woman, but this is a middle-aged woman.

"Good morning, Miss Hally," Dora greets, going to her seat.

"Morning, Princess," I say with a smile on my face.

I smile at the woman. "Morning."

"I am Bryan's housekeeper," she replies.

I let out a sigh then stretch my hand out for a shake. "It's nice to meet you.

"It is nice to meet you, too," she replies as we shake hands. "I have to go now. I'll be back at three to come to pick her up."

I nod my head and wave at her as she leaves the class. I am beginning to get worried now. I expected Bryan, not his housekeeper, to be here with Dora . *Did it end after that night at KB restaurant?* I want to hear from Bryan again, so I pick up my phone to text him.

Morning, Bryan, you know, I've been wondering why you're not here with Dora. I am missing you already. Have a beautiful day at work. I hope to see you again soon.

Bryan

A ping comes from my phone- there's a text message from Eliza. I start to read it with a smile on my face. I read it over and over again until I can see every single word with my eyes closed. Eliza is on my mind. I hope to see her soon too. I couldn't make it to the school today because I had to be at work early, but I planned to go to her house after work to see her. I feel a tap on my shoulder, and I look up to see Rose standing with her arms folded across her chest and a frown on her face. I turn around to see the same look on Lucky and Roy's faces.

"Bryan, are you okay?" Rose asks.

I nod my head then smile at Rose. "I'm so sorry, guys. I've been thinking about-"

"Eliza and Eliza alone," Roy cuts me off.

I nod my head, and they all laugh. "Guys, I can't hide it anymore. I'm in love with Eliza, and it is driving me crazy."

Lucky leaves his seat then stands before me. "Bravo! Now, you're going to join the squad of married men. Have you told her yet? I mean, have you expressed your feelings to her? Have you told her you like her?"

I shake my head. "No, I haven't. We went out on a date, and that was the last time I saw her. I didn't tell her how I feel about her, but I am sure she knows."

"You mean, you didn't tell her anything, and you want her to know how you feel," Rose says. "You're not the only man out there that likes her. Bryan, you're going to lose her if you're not smart."

I don't want to lose Eliza to any other man. Eliza is so beautiful, and every man would want to have her to himself. I want her to be mine.

"Bryan, you have to take your chance now or never. Eliza has been married, and her marriage didn't work out well. You have to prove to her that it is worth being in love again," Lucky adds. My friends are right; I have to go to Eliza.

After work, I leave for Eliza's house, not to pick Dora, but to see Eliza. Dora must be at home now with Miss Coker. I am at Eliza's house now. I knock on her door, but there is no answer. I am beginning to get worried and uneasy. The door opens suddenly, and I see Eliza right before me. As soon as she sees me, she runs into my arms and hugs me tightly. I wrap my arms around her waist slowly. I can feel my cock hardening in my trousers, and I want more than a hug. She is a plus-size lady, but she is like a baby in my arms now. Now, she is looking into my eyes with her arms wrapped around my neck. I plant a kiss on her forehead. She smiles and takes her hands off me.

"Would you like to go somewhere?" I ask.

"Are we going to another restaurant?"

I hold her hand now and shake my head. "No."

She looks confused now. "Okay. So you don't want to tell me where you're taking me?"

I nod my head and draw her hand to my mouth to kiss it.

She continues, "What about the kids? I still have three of them in the house, and they are asleep right now." She looks at her watch. "It's five already."

"And you don't want to go?"

She remains silent for a few minutes then shakes her head. "I will go. Hold on a sec while I change my dress. Jane is asleep too. I'm just going to tell her to take care of the kids."

I nod happily and let go of her hand. I watch as she returns inside with her hips swaying. With a broad smile on my face, I return to my car to wait for her. A few minutes later, she comes walking towards me. She is in a short white dress that makes her look sexy. I hurry out of my car then go to the other side to get the door open. With a smile on her face, she hops into the car while I hurriedly return to my seat and drive off.

Eliza

After driving for about forty minutes, he pulls the car to a halt by the roadside. Now, I'm beginning to wonder where we are. Bryan is always coming up with romantic surprises, so this must be somewhere special. "Where is this place, Bryan?"

He turns to look at me. "You're going to find out soon." He hops out of his car and quickly turns to the other side to open the door. He takes my hand and gently pulls me out of the car. We both start to walk towards a beautiful bamboo gate. There are four men in uniform at the gate.

"Hi," one of the men greets with a smile on his face.

"Hi, two tickets, please," Bryan replies, and the man hands two admission tickets over to us. The gate opens, and we both go inside. What I see amazes me.

"Wow!" I exclaim at the sight of the beautiful sight before us. Bryan takes my hand, and we move up the cliff until we can see the wavy water. "Bryan, this is so beautiful."

He chuckles. "I call this place, Love Cliff. This is my first time here too, but I knew about it a long time ago, and I've always wanted to come here with someone special- and here I am with that special someone."

I am beginning to blush now. I can no longer hide my happiness. With Bryan, every day is special. I've never been treated like this before. "Thank you, Bryan. I love this place so much."

He nods his head, and the next thing I feel is his arms wrapped around my waist, and his lips settle on mine in a deep kiss. It's been a long time since I've been kissed, and it feels like I am kissing for the first time. He strokes my hair with his fingers gently as we continue to kiss. I wrap my arms around his neck to draw him closer to me. I want to feel him. I can feel his hard cock pressing against my belly now. There is a sopping wet heat between my thighs, and I want to make him feel it, but that's impossible- we are outside. We are the only ones here, but this isn't the right place to go wild. I let go of his lips and open my eyes slowly. He opens his eyes too, and we both smile at each other. I turn my gaze to the wavy water. "I would love to come here again someday with you."

He grabs my hand gently, and we are standing next to each other.

"I would love to come here with you forever," I say, staring at the water.

The word *forever* makes my body tingle. I want to have Bryan by my side forever and never let go.

He continues, "Eliza, I want to be with you for the rest of my life. I want to show you what love means if you give me a chance. I knew right from the first day I met you at the school that fate has something special to offer us. You're the woman of my dreams, Eliza. I don't ever want to lose you. I want to wake up with you next to me every morning. I want to have more beautiful kids with you. I want to-"

I interrupt him by pulling him closer to me for another kiss. He grabs my waist again and slips his tongue into my mouth. *Yes, Bryan, I want to be with you. I want to wake up next to you every morning. Yes, Bryan, I want to have beautiful kids with you. Yes! Yes!! Yes!!!*

After kissing for a few minutes, we leave the cliff. Bryan drives me back to my house then leaves for his house.

CHAPTER 8

<u>Bryan</u>

After the evening at the coastal cliff, it's like Eliza and I have become inseparable. Our love story is four weeks old already, but it's like we have been dating for four years. We know almost everything about each other- I know when she is happy, and I know when to brighten her up whenever she is sad. As for Dora, she seems to like Eliza around me. Eliza's presence in my life has changed a lot of things about me; now, I know how to treat a lady like a queen, and I know how to manage my job and my relationship. I'm not going to give Eliza up for anything.

Right now, I am driving to Eliza's house. I am going to pick her up for dinner. I pull my car to a halt right in front of her house, and as I am about to hop out of my car, I see her; she is in a short red dress, and she is as beautiful as ever. She walks to the other side of my car with a smile on her face. As soon as she enters the car,

I grab her neck gently and pull her closer for a kiss. I am about to start the car, but she holds my hand.

"Bryan, I want you," she whispers, looking straight into my eyes.

I smile at her. We have never had sex, and I have been waiting for the moment. I nod my head and turn on the ignition of my car then drive straight to my house. As soon as we get to my house, I see Miss Coker, coming out of the house with Dora.

"Hello, Eliza. Oh, Bryan, thank goodness you're here," Miss Coker says, walking towards us.

"Where are you guys going?" I ask, looking at Dora.

"We are going to my house, and we will be back tomorrow morning. I called you, but you didn't pick up," Miss Coker replies.

"I'm sorry, I didn't hear my phone ring," I reply.

Dora comes closer to me and holds my hand. "Dad, I made new friends at Miss Coker's house."

I turn to look at Miss Coker. "Is that true?"

Miss Coker nods her head. "Yes, Bryan, my sister's kids are around. They are three girls."

"Oh, that's good," I say, smiling.

"We will be back tomorrow morning," Miss Coker says.

"Alright, you're good to go," I say and bend forward to plant a kiss on Dora's forehead.

"Bye, Dora," Eliza says and hugs Dora.

Dora leaves with Miss Coker happily. Hand-in-hand, Eliza and I head straight to my room.

Eliza

We are in his room now. I start to look around the beautiful room. This is my first time in his room, and I am so happy to be here. We remain silent for a while before I finally break the silence.

"Do you sleep here with Dora?" I start, still looking around the room. I want him inside of me, I want to feel him so strong in me, but I want him to make a move first.

"No, her room is next to mine," he replies.

I nod my head. "Okay."

"So, do you want anything? I'm a good cook, you know," he asks, giggling.

"I'm okay. I want a cup of water," I reply, smiling. Bryan plants a kiss on my forehead then moves out of the room to get me water. Bryan, can we get started already? I am beginning to think Bryan is a virgin, and he doesn't know how to start, but no, he isn't a virgin. He has a child, and he had told me a lot about his sex life. *Why do we feel awkward around each other now? We had just agreed a few minutes ago before heading to his house that we will be having sex, but now there is an awkward silence between us.*

Bryan returns a few minutes later with a cup of water in his hand. He hands it to me, and I gulp it down hurriedly. I hand the cup over to Bryan, and we stare into each other's eyes. We stand and stare at each other for a while without uttering a word. I clear my throat to break this awkward silence. Bryan walks up to me, crowding me against the wall, and the next thing I feel is his lips on mine. This kiss is different from the ones we've had - a kiss that makes you feel something special is about to happen next. He unzips my dress hurriedly with one hand and pulls my bra off. Still kissing, he cups my tit in his hand. I moan with pleasure as I feel his hardened cock pressed against my belly. He starts to unbutton his shirt hurriedly until he is bare-chested before me. With one hand and with my eyes closed, I unzip his pants and pull them off. I can feel his naked cock in my hand now. He moans as he cups my ass in his hands and lifts me lightly. I wrap my legs around his waist.

"I love you, Eliza, promise you're going to be with me forever," he whispers, and I can feel unspeakable sensual promise in his voice.

I moan and look into his eyes as pleasure engulfs me. "I promise, I promise, Bryan."

He lays me gently on the bed and sinks to his knees between my thigh and starts placing soft kisses on the skin of my inner thigh. I throw my head back and moan with pleasure as he moves higher and higher until I can feel his tongue on my clit. I moan loudly at the feeling of his warm tongue on my clit.

He raises his head and looks into my eyes with his hands in my hands. "Baby, I want to get us a condom."

"You don't have to, Bryan. We've got no worries. We're safe."

He smiles at me and kisses my forehead softly. "Thank goodness, baby. I promise we are both going to enjoy this moment."

I nod my head slowly and close my eyes as we begin to ride into ecstasy.

CHAPTER 9

Eliza

"Wake up, wake up," I hear Bryan say. I open my eyes slowly to see him smiling next to me. He bends lower and kisses me on the lips.

"Morning," I reply, yawning. "What time is it?"

"Seven," he replies. "Thank God it's Saturday. You're free today."

"Yeah," I reply tiredly and close my eyes slowly. We had sex last night, and it was like it wasn't going to end. I feel his lips on mine again, and I open my eyes with a smile on my face.

"Wake up, baby," he says, pulling my hand.

I burst into laughter. "Oh, Bryan, let me be. I want to get some more sleep."

"You're not going to sleep- not when I'm awake," he says defiantly, still smiling.

I sit up, pulling the blanket over my head. "Now, I'm awake."

"I made us breakfast. Should we have it in bed?"

I nod my head slowly. "Yes, I want to have breakfast in bed, Bryan."

He pulls the blanket off my face and smiles at me again before leaving the room. My phone begins to ring- it's Jane. I pick up the call and raise the phone to my ear.

"Morning, Jane."

"Morning, Sweetheart, are you still at Bryan's house?"

"Yes, I am, but I'll be back soon."

"Alright, huh, a parent came here a few minutes ago."

"But, we have no kids in the house."

"Yeah, she said she wants to see you. She wouldn't tell me why, but she looks dangerous. I've never seen her before."

"Did she tell you her name?"

"No, she didn't. I was so scared when she got here. Please come home soon."

"Alright, I will. I'll be home soon. Don't be scared, okay?"

"Okay, talk to you later," she says and disconnects the call. I am so worried about Jane now. No parent has ever been to my house on a Saturday, and Jane is familiar with every parent that comes to pick up their child at my house.

Bryan enters with a tray in his hand. "I made us sandwiches and coffee. Do you want some milk in your coffee?"

"Yeah, I want some milk," I reply worriedly.

Bryan sets the tray on the bed and sits next to me. "You look worried, babe. Are you okay?"

I nod my head then sit up. "Yes, I am. I'm fine."

"Are you sure there's nothing wrong?"

"Yes, I'm sure. Everything is fine. Bryan, I have to leave now."

"Why? I thought you planned to stay here until Dora returns?"

I nod my head slowly. "Yes, but I have to be with Jane now. She is missing me."

"Are you sure this is about Jane only?" he asks worriedly.

"Yeah, can I get the coffee?"

Bryan hands the cup of coffee over to me, and I begin to drink it. I am so worried, and all I can think about is Jane and the strange parent that was at my house a few minutes ago. *Keep calm, Eliza, it could be one of the parents who want you to take care of their kids after school.*

After eating, I start to get dressed hurriedly.

"Hold on, babe, while I take my bath and drive you back to your house," Bryan says, walking towards the bathroom.

I shake my head. "No, Bryan, I can't wait any longer."

"I'm not going to spend ten minutes in the bathroom. You know, I have to take my bath and head straight to work."

I sigh heavily then walk closer to him to plant kisses on his cheeks. "No, Bryan, I'll be fine. You have to wait for Dora to come back. She is going to be mad at you if she doesn't see you in the house."

"Alright, babe, will you go in my car? You can have the keys," he offers then holds my hand.

I shake my head. "No, thank you, I'm going to take a taxi, and I'll be fine."

He smiles at me and lets go of my hand. I carry my bag and rush out of the house to the street. Two minutes later, a car stops right before me.

"Hello, Miss Hally," a young lady in the car greets mw with a smile on her face.

I have never seen her before, and I am surprised that she knows my name. There is a man next to her in the car too.

The lady continues, "My bad, I'm so sorry. I am Maria's aunt. Maria is one of your students. We are heading towards TC Avenue, and I am sure that's where you stay."

I nod my head. Maria is one of my students, but I don't know much about Maria's family. I only know Maria's father, and I have never seen her mother. I nod my head then open the door and get in the car. The next thing I see is the young lady pointing a gun at me.

"Who the hell are you?" I ask, trembling.

"Hush, keep quiet, or I'm going to blow your head off," the lady threatens. I remain quiet and keep staring at them with fright.

Bryan

Dora and Miss Coker return a few minutes after Eliza has left the house.

"Morning, Dad," Dora greets.

"Morning, Bryan, you're ready for work?" Miss Coker asks.

"Yeah," I reply and plant a kiss on Dora's forehead before leaving the house. I get in my car and start to drive to work. My phone rings; it's Anita. I pick up the call and wait for her to start. *What does she want this time? If she wants Dora, I'm not going to let her take her. Dora is a part of me now.*

"Hello, Bryan," she greets with a husky voice.

"Hello, Anita, how may I help you?"

"Huh? No sexy word for the mother of your child?"

I roll my eyes with disgust. "What do you want?"

"It's simple. Well, I have the one you love the most, so let's talk business."

My heart skips a beat. She is not talking about Dora because I left Dora a few minutes ago. I have not called Eliza yet to ask if she is home. "What are you talking about, Anita?"

She chuckles over the phone. "Well, Eliza is with me."

My body begins to tremble. "Anita, what do you want from me? You have to let her go right now."

"Now, you're talking, Bryan. I know you love her so much, and you will do anything for her. Hold on a sec; let me put her on the line." The next thing I hear is Eliza's screams.

"I'm back, Bryan. You heard Eliza quite well, Bryan. I have her, and if you want her out of my den, you have to get $10,000 paid into my account. You have only twenty-four hours or else I blow her head off. Don't play smart with me, Bryan, because you're never going to get me. I know that you're a detective, but don't act like one when you're dealing with me."

"What the hell!" I exclaim then remain silent for a few minutes before concluding. "Alright, Anita, I am going to give you money, but please don't hurt her."

Anita chuckles over the phone. "I'm not going to hurt her if I get my money. Bryan, twenty-four hours is all you've got," she concludes and disconnects the call. I turn around and drive back home. I have to make the payment as soon as possible. I don't want to put Eliza's life in danger because of me. I want to tell my friends about it, but Anita already warned me; she doesn't want me to include anyone. Anita is dangerous, and I don't want Eliza's life to be at risk. I get to my house and start to make arrangements for the payment. I can do anything for Eliza; I am going to do anything for her.

CHAPTER 10

<u>Eliza</u>

Today is my third day here without food. The only thing she offers me is water. I am so weak, and I keep praying for a miracle. I know Bryan is going to get me out of here soon. I don't know why I am here. The lady who claimed to be Maria's aunt wouldn't allow me to talk to her. I tried to ask her the questions running through my mind, but she wouldn't let me speak. I am in a dark room with no one with me. A few minutes later, I hear the door open, and I hear footsteps approaching. I don't know who it is yet because the room is too dark for me to see clearly. The person flashes a light at me, and I use my arms to cover my eyes.

"Hi, Eliza, I know you must be wondering why you're still here. It's been three days now, and I have kept you away from the outside world. Well, my name is Anita, and I am Dora's mother. You must have heard a lot about me, so no more introductions," she says then moves closer to me and wraps her arm around my neck. "I know Bryan likes you, and I am not going to hurt you. I asked him for a ransom of $10,000. To my utmost surprise, he paid it all within twenty-four hours. Isn't that romantic of him? Poor boy, he loves you so much." She chuckles and takes her hand off me now then takes a few steps away from me. "You know what, Eliza? I want more money, and I want $150,000 this time. He will do anything for you, won't he? You know, I started all of this when I noticed that Bryan doesn't want to have anything to do with me. He didn't even send me money; neither did he call to ask after me. I had to take this step to get money from him."

She takes her hand off me now and takes a few steps away from me.

"He is going to get it for you," she concludes and leaves the room. I am beginning to wonder how Bryan is going to get all of that because of me. I don't even have that in my account.

Bryan

Since Eliza's abduction, I have not been happy. Anita wouldn't let Eliza go. After paying her the sum of $10,000, she wants me to get $150,000, which is quite a lot for me to pay. I have $130,000 in my bank account, and I will be left with nothing if I give that to Anita. Who knows if she is going to request more? I haven't told my friends about it yet because I am scared of losing Eliza. I have not been going to work since Eliza's abduction, and my colleagues have been calling to know what's up with me. I am in my house with Dora, Jane, and Miss Coker. I told them what happened, and they are both as sad as I am right now.

"What do we do now, Bryan? I mean, you're not going to remain in this house without taking a step," Miss Coker says worriedly.

"Dad, I want Miss Hally," Dora cries.

"I think we should involve the police now. We can't continue this way. Who knows if Eliza is still alive or not? I am scared, Bryan. Eliza is all I've got right now," Jane says sobbing.

"Bryan, you have to involve the police. Please, do this for us," Miss Coker says, wrapping her arms around Dora.

I stand up immediately and leave the house without saying a word. I have to tell my friends now. I have to do it. I am sure they are going to start searching for her immediately. As soon as I get to the office, I tell my friends and the chief everything, and we begin an investigation immediately.

"Anita is in an abandoned warehouse on LIGO Avenue, and I am sure that's where she is going to keep Eliza," Roy says, reading from the computer screen before him.

"We don't have to waste time. Let's get moving," Rose says, and we all leave the office for LIGO Avenue with five more detectives. An hour later, we get to LIGO Avenue and head straight to the old abandoned warehouse. We are outside the deserted warehouse now.

"Guys, this place is so old and too dry. I don't think there's anyone here," I say, looking confused.

"This place is big enough to accommodate five hundred persons, Bryan," Rose whispers. A few minutes later, we enter the dusty warehouse and start to search. There are several rooms in the warehouse. After searching the rooms, we move upstairs to check the rooms there. We open the door to the third room and turn our flashlights on. To my utmost surprise, I see Eliza curled up on the floor. I walk towards her and carry her in my arms.

"Thank God you're here, Bryan," Eliza cries and wraps her arms around my neck.

I kiss her forehead gently with tears welling up in my eyes. "I'm so sorry, Eliza."

Just when we are about to leave the warehouse, we see Anita approaching. As soon as she sees us, she tries to run, but Rose and Roy get hold of her and lead her into the car. I offer to drive Eliza to the hospital, but she says she is going to be okay, and I should take her home. I drive her straight to my house. As soon as Dora, Jane, and Miss Coker see her, they all run into her arms for a hug.

As soon as they let go of her, I move closer to her and wrap my hands around her waist. "Marry me, Eliza."

Miss Coker and Jane clap and cheer happily.

"Dad, where is the ring? Aren't you supposed to get her one?" Dora asks, and we all burst into laughter.

"I don't have a ring yet, but I am going to get one soon. Eliza, I want us to get married soon. I can't bear to lose you again. Please, don't say no."

Eliza nods her head with a smile on her face. "Yes, Bryan, I will."

Dora, Miss Coker, and Jane clap and shout happily as we kiss.

EPILOGUE

A Year Later

Eliza

We got married two months ago, and we have been living together like we have been together for many years. I am so happy for making the right choice. Finally, I am with the man of my dreams. With Bryan, I have been able to achieve every goal of mine.

My desktop computer is before me. I am trying to figure out a name for my school, and I am preparing for its launch in the next two weeks. I am going to own a school soon- thanks to my husband, who has helped me to achieve my dreams. I stopped working at KB Elementary school a week after my wedding.

Bryan and Dora enter with two shopping bags in their hands. Dora comes running towards me.

"Oh, baby, you're back," I say, taking her into my arms.

"Yes, Miss Hally, I got you ice-cream and chocolates," she says, smiling and handing one of the bags over to me.

"Oh, my princess got me chocolate and ice-cream," I reply happily. Dora runs to her room, leaving Bryan and me in the living-room.

Bryan comes closer to me and wraps his arms around my waist and kisses my neck softly. "You know, with you, I am the luckiest man on earth."

I giggle as sensation runs through my body.

He continues, "Guess what? Dora is going to be the first to be admitted to your school."

"What? She is leaving KB?"

Bryan nods his head. "Yeah, she wants to be in your school."

"That's so sweet of her, Bryan."

"Yes."

"Guess what, Bryan."

"What?"

"I have a name for my school already."

"Huh, I want to know what it is, please."

"DEB. DEB Elementary school."

"DEB Elementary school? What does DEB mean?"

"Dora, Eliza, and Bryan."

"Wow! That's so sweet," Bryan says and carries me in his arms happily. "I love you, Eliza. You're the best decision I've ever made."

I chuckle. "I love you too, Bryan."

Thank you for reading my book!

Be the first to know about new releases, giveaways and other special contents! Find my books in all major online book stores!

9 798636 736363